DEMOS RISING

Edited by Isabelle Kenyon

First published October 2022 by Fly on the Wall Press
Published in the UK by
Fly on the Wall Press
56 High Lea Rd
New Mills
Derbyshire
SK22 3DP

www.flyonthewallpress.co.uk
ISBN: 9781913211905
Copyright remains with individual authors © 2022

Contents

Extinction Rebellion, London Occupation April 2019
Leslie Tate

With acknowledgments to Adlestrop, Edward Thomas

I remember
where we nested on trucks
with our talons drilled into metal
as we sent up wild cries calling to our children,
and they gathered,
rising from their bedrooms
and playgrounds and schoolrooms
to fold their wings around the wounds
and consecrated body of Earth, our host.

How we made tarmac into garden,
seeding ourselves in the night
and easing up next morning
through drains and cracks
to release soft balsamic fragrance
and love-repeat blooms
unlocking who we are.

Yes, I remember how we offered ourselves,
sitting cross-legged on stony ground
held together by our songbooks and testimonies
and the rising tide of quiet
on the bridge and in the Square,
and in the silent wait at the Circus for leaf-boat rescue.

And in that minute, as I watched, the air became an Arch,
the sun told the truth; the traffic stopped
and the trees and protestors stood tall
raising a dream-song space with their bodies,
while all the birds
of Oxfordshire and Gloucestershire
sang emergency.

Unite
Nigel Kent

They call him the Poet of the Placard,
the Political Punster, the People's Sloganeer;
the marshal of those hordes of words
he calls upon to demonstrate, irritate, humiliate.
He's the man ministers love to hate
for stripping bare their dressed up lies
to march them naked through the streets,
exposing to the few (bold enough to look)
the ugliness beneath their tailored suits.
With rhyme and reason, he turns
their fickle words against them,
puts their probity on public trial
and prosecutes with precise wit
though he knows even the severest
sentence will not take them down:
they'll carry on the same,
for words are but puffs of wind;
it takes thousands of voices speaking
as one to blow the hurricane
that will bring them to their knees.

Still Warm
Viv Fogel

For murdered Myanmar poet/activist Khet Thi 1976 – 2021

They clawed out his heart   threw it
on a slab with his other organs,
sent it back in a jar.

What did they hope to learn?
How fierce with fight and protest?
How fearless?

> *"They try to bury us—but they don't know*
> *we are the seeds."*

A megaphone for the silenced
his poems gave voice to those
in fear, urged them on

What could his heart say now? Severed
from breath, its longing faint
its words turning grey?

> *"They shoot us in the head, but they don't know*
> *that revolution dwells in the heart."*

Cut loose, his poetheart soars above,
drums down the darkening rage
the warrior's thunder—

Listen   it is trying to tell you
how to love—can you hear it
pounding?

A Prayer for Peace
Viv Fogel

May peace surround you
                    —let the air be clear of sniper shots and sirens
May peace be above you
                    —and the sky be free of missiles and mortar
May peace be beneath you
             —not the cautious tread through the ruins of your broken city

Peace be behind you
          —not the mute children clutching their mum's coat, babe in arms,
     picking paths through bricks, burnt out car wreckage, bomb-shelled school.

Peace be to your left
   —not what is left: your shattered home, your parents who beg you to leave.

Peace be to your right
          —not the loss of rights, to choose to stay, to fight, to flee, to survive.

Peace be before you
              —not the wobble over hard-pitted snow and uneven tracks,
           the long cold wait for visas, video calls, the brutal uncertainty.

Peace be within you
          —like the warmth of a cup and blanket handed you at the border,
       the sudden smile or dazzle of sunlight through a dust-streaked pane,
          or the voice of your loved ones, when you finally get a signal.

May peace follow you
              —wherever you find yourself, and live inside you
                 like the heartbeat of an unborn child

Voice
Barsa Ray

Amma and I stand in the line. There are many people before us. We've been waiting for ages and my legs feel heavy. I try to sit down but Amma won't let go of my hand. I tug hard. She looks at me then and picks me up.

Abba has gone to get water, but I won't drink any. Poor Bobo is all alone. He'll be thirsty too. Abba made me leave him behind. He must be so scared. I cried and cried when we got on the boat. Why did Abba say I couldn't bring Bobo? I saw a girl who brought her teddy bear. I look for the girl, but she's lost somewhere. My eyes are heavy. I rest my head on Amma's shoulder.

When I open my eyes, I see Abba's arms, his curly hair under his kufi. He's carrying me! I kick out. He tries to calm me but I hit at his face till he puts me down. I take off. I run and run till I can't breathe. My feet stumble. I come to a stop. There's dust everywhere. People everywhere. No Amma. I walk towards where I think they were, but can't see them. I can't call out so I cry. I go up to women who look like Amma. They're not her. Then suddenly I hear Abba's voice.

"Imi, Imi!"

I run like mad towards him. He swings me up.

"They have accepted us. You can rest now."

I have been sleeping, on your shoulder, I sign.

He laughs and kisses me.

"God is merciful. We made a safe passage. We can start over. I'll get you another teddy."

I look at him. He doesn't understand. Bobo was my voice. Without him no one will hear me.

11

The Battle of Euston
by Rachel Swabey

In the pulsing heart of England's most sprawling concrete jungle, amid beeping cars, buzzing skyscrapers and the constant rushing drama of human existence, we crouch within the earth. It's quiet down here; the dirt packed above us muffles the roar of traffic, the scuffles with police, the drone of chainsaws. But, in some ways, it feels closer to real life than it does up there on the surface.

Down here we're hyper-aware of our bodies, the shape and size and smells of ourselves as we contort to get past each other, to gather in small huddles, to play cards, share food, keep each other sane, or as we stretch out to try and sleep or to read by the pallid glow of a phone. Our bashed-up old generator affords us that concession to modernity. We're growing used to the constant all-over ache from endless hours spent hunched and crawling.

Time's different too. Tunnel time. There are no changes in light to mark night and day—the only external marker of time is the bailiffs changing shifts as they take it in turns to try and dig us out—unless we visit the downshaft, blinking up at the daylight like moles.

But we're not moles, are we? We are The Badgers. Badgers fighting pigs. Like this is a forest, like it's an ecosystem. Not that we really see the pigs down here. It's the surface dwellers—our squirrel cousins trying desperately to protect the trees up in the park—who wrestle with them. The bailiffs sniffing around our tunnel are an entirely different animal. Which creatures are they in the tangled branches of this forest metaphor? Foxes, maybe? They're certainly sly bastards. And diggers. They've dug their own downshaft alongside ours.

But in real life the forces acting on the institutionalised souls up there are far from natural. It's easy to feel like prey down here, to cast them as predators closing in, but it's a much more complicated dance than that, a far stranger symbiosis. They take our shit away, the bailiffs. Not as in they take our stuff, although they'd do that too given half a chance. No, they literally take away our shit in buckets. Health and safety.

And even as they hunt us down, they take pains not to hurt us too badly. We know some of them want to. Others couldn't give two shits— they're 'just doing their jobs'. Either way, they're going against their natures. What stops them hurting us is fear of bad press—how's that for a human concept? And yet, that bad press is what we're here for. So you could say the forces acting on us aren't natural either. But still, here we are: in nature, for nature, as nature. Living in this unnatural, hunched-up, lightless way, nature's last line of defence.

Did you know that trees talk to each other by sending chemical messages through their roots? We were talking about it the other day, as chainsaws droned above us and the carcasses of the trees that stood there piled up. They form communities, nurture the weak and warn each other of danger through a giant web of fungi scientists are calling the Wood Wide Web.

And we spoke about the other networks vying for dominance in the complex clamour that is human life in the twenty-first century: the massive new road-building plan that's been in the news; HS-bloody-2; 'wildlife corridors' (because that's all that's left now: corridors); linked-up humans, sharing, arguing, building, ever more connected and ever more divided. We spoke about Covid spreading through human contact and the ecosystems we mostly ignore, but on which our lives depend, some destroyed forever, some hanging stubbornly on.

Then there's us: the badgers. How do we fit in? Increasingly, we've been cut off from our wider support networks as we're forced deeper underground, but in a funny way, the forces of all those other networks seem to collide in our makeshift tunnel system as our story ripples out into the world.

Yesterday, Lazer locked himself on at the base of the downshaft, to a steel tube encased in concrete. For hours, the bailiffs drilled, manhandling him at every opportunity. How he stood it we don't know, although we like to think we'd all have done the same in his position. We did chuckle, though, when we realised the bailiffs' equipment was all battery powered, so they had to keep stopping to recharge. They didn't like that.

A video of one of the bailiffs sitting on him has gone viral. As has a picture we snapped after they drilled Lazer's arm tube out of its concrete casing. He managed to slip away from them before they could get him out, the tube still attached to his forearm. You can see it in the picture. The other hand is sticking two fingers up as he grins triumphantly, eyes bright.

"Lazer beaming," we chuckled.

For an hour or so after he came back down, he was a celebrity. We clambered over each other—quite literally—to commend his bravery, to hug him, to bask in his elation. Then he was absorbed back into our number. Just another badger.

We cracked open a jar of olives to celebrate his escape and a few hours later, as the excitement subsided, we began to sing. It's hard to tell how it started; it wasn't so much an idea as an unspoken primal force. We closed our eyes to the darkness, let our heads fill with the harmony of shared purpose, and fell into the rhythm of each other.

Imagine A Bomb
Colin Dardis

after F.E. McWilliam's Woman in a Bomb Blast, 1974

You can't imagine a bomb.

Watch the news, note the aftermath:
exposed brickwork, burnt-out cars,
nameless citizens crying.

The camera will never tell you
of the blood, nurseries now graves,
the blown-off limb just out of shot,

never detailing the seconds of heat
and noise that strips a bystander
of their clothes, then their life.

No help coming to those still alive
by miracle or missed target, everyone else
dead, or at home, watching TV.

Imagine this is your world.
The manufacturers don't imagine this.
They imagine three billion pounds

of annual turnover, each note
cleaned of collateral damage
and resting in bomb-proof vaults.

Death doesn't come from the sky
but from a production line
in the United Kingdom.

Round Black Grains
Kevin Doyle

At his wake, we talked about the time Justin nearly died in the Glen, trying to save the sand martins. Really, what was he thinking? The colony of birds had been living in the urban wilderness for as long as anyone could remember, their nests long tunnels burrowed into the sandy deposits left behind when the glaciers receded.

A consortium, *Skellig Developments*, planned to build houses beside this ancient abode, only to discover that the birds enjoyed protection under some obscure bylaw. They proposed a solution, a compromise it was called, to build the sand martins a new home, a short distance from where they had always lived. These units, concrete towers bristling with hollow plastic pipes, were superior to sand dunes apparently—studies had showed. They didn't suffer from the damp; they were durable and they could even be painted to appear as if they were part of the surrounding terrain.

The city council was thrilled. Finding itself mired in an ethical dilemma of stupendous proportions—could progress run roughshod over these ancient dwellers?—they finally saw a way out. Voting to lift the injunction, they accepted the generous offer from Skellig and, a few days later, the new towers were hauled into position.

That night a strange contraption also appeared in the Glen, blocking access to the site. It had three spindly legs intersecting four meters above the ground. Hanging from the apex of this structure was a tiny capsule not unlike a chair-o-plane seat. Sitting in this was Justin.

A garda explained. He had seen the structure before, a tripod it was called, at an anti-Shell Oil protest in Mayo. It was designed to interdict the movement of ground vehicles along narrow lanes and roadways. It couldn't easily be moved, in fact assistance would have to be summoned.

This arrived shortly. From a van that said 'Garda Specialist Unit', three police officers dressed in black alighted and filmed the scene. Their peaked baseball caps read G.S.U. and they had with them a dune buggy that they went around in for a while, mostly up and down the narrow track obstructed by the tripod. They examined the obstacle, took pictures with telescopic lens and rattled its spindly legs. They ascertained through a combination of measurements and stress tests that Justin's abode was structurally sound. A cherry picker was sent for and duly arrived—rented, it later emerged from a subsidiary of Skellig's called *Skellig Equipment*. We jeered and sang songs, held away at a distance as we were from the stand-off by a robust chain link fence.

15

The strange thing, though, was the sand martins. We could see them in the distance. In the beginning they had scattered in squalls—there was quite a population of them—but as the day progressed, as the crowd of onlookers grew, the entire colony of birds took up a stationary position on the sandy cliff face.

The garda unit were serious men. Two went into the cherry picker cabin, while a third videoed proceedings. The picker rose like a serpent's head and drew level with the capsule. Some time was spent talking to Justin, reasoning with him, but apparently—we read this later in the newspaper, the one that described us as rent-a-mob—he couldn't be reasoned with. So eventually battle lines were drawn and pepper spray used. It was a sight: seeing the tripod rock from side to side, Justin swinging wildly in the capsule. Finally, he was extracted and brought down, escorted to a position near the builder's hut. He was offered tea and informed that he wouldn't be arrested. Apparently *Skellig Developments* had endured enough adverse publicity.

Divested of its human inhabitant, a bulldozer moved forward and smashed the tripod into the ground. Earth movers followed on then quickly, trundling up the narrow road towards the dunes. We saw a JCB's claw rise into the air and swipe wildly at the tallest of these. The sand martins flew away, scattering into the air as a tall wedge of sand separated from the cliff face and toppled.

In the hiatus that followed, knowing that his cause was lost, Justin broke free again. Dodging gardaí and a variety of *Skellig* goons, he ran forward and dived into a collapsing heap of sand. It seemed to take forever before it was understood what had happened. Gardaí and *Skellig* employees ran to help. Anger followed panic. Shouts of 'madman' and 'who does he think he is?', could be heard. The JCB driver was livid and the first to claw at the mound. There were fears of another collapse but that stopped nobody. Within a few minutes Justin's head of black hair was located. A vent space to his mouth was cleared next and after that his shoulders were released. It was only a matter of time then. They excavated quickly, uncovering a figure contorted around his own cupped hands. As he was finally pulled free, he shouted, spluttering his sandy words:

"Gentle please, gentle. Mind the birds."

There's a photo of the moment—on *Indymedia*. A collection of men in orange hi-vis vests and white helmets are gathered around Justin. In his lap, nestled for protection, is a sand martin chick. The fledgling was so frightened she had withdrawn her head deep into her body. Her neck had vanished, her eyes were round black grains.

Wound
Zarah Alam
For the Earth's lost daughters

knife shoved between taut, tan thighs / trembling/ tiny/ told lies to get her
to lie/ open wide/ lips part/ eyebrows crease/ heart breaks with every beat/
again/ it nears/ blunt rusty blade, barely shining in the heat/ weapon of women
wielded by women/ remnants of the last theft stubbornly cling in splotches of
maroon and stains of pink/ she is flesh/ just flesh/ to be cut and prepared/ for a
man too old/ ancient/ heart beats with every break/ the screams repeat, forever
on loop/ leaves them reeling/ who's next?/ next knife in/ screams sound this
season/ the chorus/ crescendo/ this season of cutting and looting/ for a small
red pearl the size of a teardrop/ for a precious gem which excuses intrusion/
no/ not precious/ evil/ a stain on perfection/ but God-given, so surely nothing
but perfection?/ no/ no woman born pure/ must be purified/ or else whores/
look at those countries/ open-legged/ loose women/ must be stitched closed/
stand up straight/ legs closed/ for the shame/ the shame/ shame no penalty
placed/ time for the daughter to taste the truth of her birthright/ is this right?/
yes/ can't stop now/ she needs breaking/ bending/ while still soft/ mold them
early/ they will listen now/ all they see, smell, hear, feel is pain/ they can't
rebel if they can't run/ invisibly visible/ openly secret/ blood blossoms beneath
bosoms/ a secret garden with a maroon pool/ pool grows into an ocean/ whole
country is drowned red/ whole world stained red/ red ruddy ground/ red
sun/ red sunset/ red sunrise/ next daughter dies/ unblinking eyes never shed
lest the dam release/ polluted with guilt and hidden shame/ with the foul
stench of stolen childhood/ for the crime committed under her blade/ traitor/
she who ruins to purify/ purges true purity/ cuts off her wings and
wonders why won't she fly?/ holds her down/ with two three four
others who are guilty/ guilty victims/ victims of guilt/ *hold her down*/ be
firmer/ try harder/ *sinful child, stop shaking!*/ *child, why do you struggle?*/
bathe in the blessing this weapon has brought/ *thank it*/ *you are now clean*

/ off you go

Deep In That Water
Beth Brooke

a poem for seven voices

Poet's Prelude

water,
the sound of something
ripping;

somewhere something is
tearing apart,

cloud covers the moon;

we cannot tell
the devils in the shadows
from the angels weeping.

We cling to one another,
don't dare to breathe;
a breath could so easily
become our tipping point.

Doaa

We paid them money and it was too late
to turn back.
They rammed the boat, holed it, said,
Let the fishes eat your flesh.
The sea went black;
people screaming, water crashing;
we almost drowned in the bodies
of the already dead.

Mahmoud

When you are poor you cannot even choose
how to escape,

I was a carpenter in Damascus, before the war.
It does not seem to matter where we ran,

death followed us everywhere,
from Misrata and into the sea.

My daughter left her words in that deep water,
and we left our son.

Afghani youth

They give you a knife,
sharp
stab—or the police will gut you, send you back

aman was all we wanted
we are not to blame

One man waded out,
brought us to land,
to land in our own tongue

aman, aman

we had no choice
bombardment or take a boat

Ghias, volunteer in Lesbos

I went on the 3rd:
laptop, ticket,
found where the boats
were coming

at the first one I left everything
bag, laptop, my everything,
went into the water to
pull them in.

There was a woman with her child
and I pulled them out of the water,
onto the beach and she said,

At home I wash my
husband's feet; why do you
kneel to me?

Maybe, I told her, it is *aman*.

Priti Patel, UK Home Secretary

The do-gooders, the lefty lawyers, the Labour Party,
all defend the indefensible;
we need to stop those people coming,
making endless legal claims to remain.
I hope that the whole House can come together,
to send a clear message that crossing the Channel
in this lethal way is not the way to come to our country.

Footnote. UNICEF

There are 5.6 million
Syrian refugees,
more than 6 million
internally displaced.
Half of these
are children.

The word aman means safety in Arabic. This poem is based on transcripts of an interview with Ghias, a Syrian living in Britain who went to Lesbos as a volunteer, on testimonies from refugees on the UNICEF, worldvision.org websites, and Priti Patel's address to the Tory Party Conference 2020 and her speech to the House of Commons in November 2021. The stanzas are a mix of verbatim and paraphrased testimony, apart from stanza one which is the poet's response to testimony from a number of refugees.

At Kramatorsk Station
Beth Brooke

The dead have left their luggage at the station,
it litters the concourse,
lies along the platforms in untidy heaps.

A child's rucksack, pink and unicorned,
rests against a wall;
there are suitcases, clothes disgorged,
the optimism of their colours
at odds with the drying blood.

There is a little knitted horse—some infant's treasure.
It waits quietly to be retrieved, scooped up by
small hands, cuddled in relief at being found.

Plastic bags of groceries—food for the
journey—are spilled, torn, already
they are beginning
to spoil.

The dead huddle, wait for the trains
they will not catch. They are bewildered,
wonder what has happened here to
make them leave so much untidily behind
at Kramatorsk station.

Where is Chandernagore?
Janet H Swinney

Umbrellas of cow parsley stood tall in the hedgerows as Enid jolted down the rutted track towards the river. The tools in the basket on her handlebars rattled and jumped as she tried to steer a steady course. Her palms were damp with sweat. She had told her father she was staying late in town for a rehearsal of maestro Verdi's *Requiem*—for which she had specifically joined the choral union—but she was on an entirely different mission.

*

Of all the students who'd graduated from Skerry's college the previous year, George Allardyce had not been one of the more accomplished. Yet, here he was, flinging his hat on to the coat-stand in the corner of the Examiner office, and unburdening himself of his overcoat in the manner of a seasoned reporter with too many places to go and not enough time to get between them.

He rubbed out a cigarette between his fingers and dropped his pad on to Enid's desk. "There you go, En."

Enid examined the pad with distaste. There were signs that a beer glass had been parked on several of the pages. "What do you call this?"

"Flick through, and you'll see me report of this morning's court proceedings. Mr. Peabody said...Tonight's edition."

"I know what Mr. Peabody said," Enid snapped.

George shot off to the gents, and Enid rolled her eyes at her colleague Hattie, seated on the other side of the desk. Hattie, several years her senior, was checking, at leisurely pace, the schedule for a series of Temperance meetings that were due to take place on the Town Moor. Enid adjusted the ribbon in her Imperial typewriter, and started typing, her wrists held high like the fetlocks of a thoroughbred horse. George's shorthand was atrocious, and his powers of analysis dim.

"Fill out the blanks," Enid sighed. Hattie cackled.

The case concerned a miner who was charged with persistent cruelty to his wife. Through the scrimmage of dots and dashes that constituted George's shorthand, Enid managed to discern that things had come to a head on the night he had 'started' on her with the poker, threatening to kill her. The miner's defence was that his wife never had his tea ready when he came home from work. She disputed this wholeheartedly and pointed out that he had recently smashed a pot over her head, and that his language was never less than foul.

George reappeared from the WC.

"So what was the verdict?"

"Pardon?"

"This case you've reported on in such eloquent detail: you haven't provided the outcome."

"Haven't I?"

"No."

"Oh, case dismissed."

"On what grounds?"

"The magistrate took the view that the wife had provoked her man beyond endurance. He said that if he separated everyone who squabbled, or where the man was inclined to cuss, there would be very few couples left together." George grabbed his hat and coat from the stand. "He had a point, I suppose," he chortled, and slammed the door behind him.

Enid finished typing and looked thoughtfully at the completed report. "You know, Hattie," she observed, "the few pleasurable moments in women's lives blind us to the fact that, on the whole, the situation is grim. Our freedom is entirely circumscribed by the whims and diktats of other people."

"Meaning?" said Hattie.

"Men."

The older woman laughed. "Oh," she said. "Now there's something new."

*

They were a shoestring enterprise. In fact, Mr. Peabody frequently referred to his bootstraps and their auspicious role in his advancement. There were other publications with far larger circulations in the city. They had reporters to send hither and yon.

"Let them focus on the big news," Mr. Peabody said. "At the Examiner, we deal with the significant detail, the family, the community."

The last court case Enid had covered had been against a lad accused of maiming a pit pony with an axe. "If his employer had provided him with a proper whip," the defence lawyer argued, "the injury would not have occurred." *What a telling detail that had been*, Enid thought, though telling her what, she wasn't quite sure. Meanwhile Hattie generally appended her byline to wholesome recipes for kidney pies and onion dumplings as well as novel designs for antimacassars. The paper did, however, provide some foreign news which they culled from the London papers and customised for belated consumption by their local readership.

24

The following morning, Mr. Peabody allocated Enid the task of drafting something about an impending spat between the French and the British somewhere west of Calcutta.

"Come on strong about the Empire quashing any interference from Johnny Foreigner," he said. "We can't have these Frenchies getting above themselves."

To Hattie, he allocated a feature about the history of milk puddings. "You can link it nicely to Enid's piece about the Empire," he said. "There's nothing like a good rice pudding with the skin on, topped with a sprinkle of nutmeg."

George, on the other hand, was given the job of covering the two-day visit of the President of the Board of Trade, Mr Winston Churchill, who would be speaking at the Assembly Rooms that very evening.

Enid was wearing her newest work blouse with starched cuffs and a clever, scalloped collar. It made her feel determined and clear-sighted. She sat upright in her chair:

"Wouldn't it be wise to send someone to cover Mr Churchill's visit who has really rapid shorthand?" she said. "If he's giving a speech about government policy, there'll be a lot of detail to get to grips with." Somehow, after a year of employment, the fact that Enid had graduated top of her Pitman's class seemed to have been entirely forgotten. Mr. Peabody looked at her blankly.

"A fat lot of good you'll do at the Assembly Rooms," said George. "You won't get in."

"Why won't she?" said Hattie. "It's a public meeting."

"Well, Mrs. Barrett, I suggest you look at the small print on the posters. It's organised by the Liberal Club and it's a public meeting for men only."

"Isn't that a contradiction in terms?" Enid started, and then changed tack. "Well, why not send two of us? Maybe those people campaigning for votes for women will be there. I'll look out for them and George can cover the speech. Then we'd have taken account of both male and female perspectives. In fact, we could do a whole spread. Hattie could postpone the puddings and do an in-depth interview with one of the suffrage leaders instead. Her life, her upbringing, her aspirations and so on. It would be a good read."

Hattie looked startled at this proposal, but no sooner had the idea begun to gain some traction with her than Mr. Peabody found his voice:

"I'm not having lasses traipsing around the streets at night. It's not right."

Enid wrinkled her nose so that her spectacles approached her eyebrows. "Surely it's a reporter's job to go where the news is?"

"Mind your lip, Enid. I've told you who's doing what."

*

Enid spun the tobacco-tinted globe in the corner of the office and, when it stopped, pressed her finger on Calcutta. Who the hell knew where Chandernagore[1] was? What's more: who cared? Was it an important place? If so, she'd never heard of it. She started on her piece: 'Just as Hexham is about 20 miles up the River Tyne from Newcastle, so is Chandernagore about 20 miles up the Hooghly from Calcutta.' She stopped. Even she thought it was pathetic. She had no information about the Hooghly river, but she was pretty sure it would be nothing like the Tyne.

"I'm going to try him again tomorrow," she said. "I can't sit here endlessly writing this drivel."

"What makes you think he'll give in?" Hattie asked.

"Don't you want to do an interview with a leading suffragette? Someone who's been in prison, maybe? Wouldn't it be exciting to get the 'inside' story from one of these women? They must have a rare tale to tell."

"I'd like to, yes."

"Then why don't we both have a go at him?"

"Because he'll get mad, and who knows where that'll lead?"

Enid found it hard not to sound exasperated. "I thought you wanted a career as a journalist. Journalists don't just sit indoors twiddling their typewriters, you know." Hattie's placid nature and elaborate handknit sweaters that had been weeks in the making irked her sometimes. Not quite cutting edge.

"I have a family to keep," said Hattie, offering Enid a barley sugar from the poke that always sat in her drawer. "I can't be gadding about all the time, the way you single women can. I need cash in hand more than I need a punt on some high-flying career."

"What I don't understand," Enid huffed, "is why he employs us at all if he's not going to use our talents. It doesn't make any business sense."

Hattie had an answer for that: "Because he's a bone-headed bigot. You're expecting logic from a man who isn't capable of it. You can rame on at him as long as you like: it's not going to do you any good."

1   *Current day Chandannagar, in the Indian state of West Bengal, formerly the admin-istrative centre of the French East India Company, but under British occupation twice during its history. Finally transferred to the Indian government in 1951.*

Enid was shocked. Her own Sunday school upbringing and intensive Bible study had led her to believe in a world in which natural justice prevailed. But here, Hattie, applying native common sense and the powers of observation, and with no more than a poke of barley sugars for reference, clearly had a shrewder grasp of the situation than she had herself.

She struggled on a little longer with her task: 'Chandernagore is a French town where the currency is British coinage. Not more than a handful of the residents actually speak the Gallic tongue'. And then she downed tools.

"I'm off," she said. "See you tomorrow."

*

The sun was already low in the winter sky as she turned into Neville Street, the nexus of the tramlines at the Westgate intersection glinting in the distance. She pulled up her coat collar and kept one gloved hand at her throat to ward off the nip in the air. Her feet ached in her stiff, leather shoes. Already, there was considerable bustle around the station. The place was thronged with women, many of them wearing sashes of purple, white and green and some wielding placards with the legend, 'Votes for Women'. But the constabulary were in evidence too, a great wall of meaty men with truncheons, patrolling the exit from platform eight where Mr Churchill's arrival was expected.

Enid edged her way towards the ticket gate. "Excuse me! Excuse me! Examiner coming through!" she proclaimed, finally securing herself a place just leeward of a hefty police sergeant and next to a woman in a fish wife's shawl. As the sense of anticipation increased, she pulled her pad from her bag and started jotting: 'Tensions rising this evening, as women of all ages, from all classes and from all walks of life assemble to greet the important Liberal politician…' She felt her heart lift in her chest. At last, she was doing the job she'd expected to do.

Finally, the locomotive trundled into the station, exhaled into the roof space and slid to a halt. Doors were flung open and passengers tumbled out on to the platform. The women craned their necks to catch sight of their quarry. And here, among the last of them, came a top-hatted gentleman. It was clear from the patrician curve of his mouth and the keen look of self-regard in his eye, that this was Churchill, a man who had experienced neither back shift nor fore shift, but who had inherited the right to pontificate about both of them. He was met by two po-faced local dignitaries who escorted him, in close formation, along the platform. The women began their choral chant: 'Votes for Women!' 'Votes for Women!' It cannoned round the great

27

gallery of the vaulted roof like an oratorio. Churchill stalked on regardless, while the women's jostling increased.

As the triumvirate passed the ticket gate, a woman thrust herself forward, waving a leaflet under Churchill's nose.

"Deeds not words!" she yelled. "Votes for women!"

Two policemen pounced immediately, wrenching the woman's arms up behind her back. More leaflets fluttered to the ground. The captive tried to detach herself from her coat to escape the officers, but they rammed her head so far forward that, soon, she was looking at her own shoelaces. "Votes for women!" she croaked. Now the crowd weighed in, forming a scrum round the policemen and bringing an assorted hail of placards, fists and umbrellas down on their shoulders. A helmet came off, a baton was flourished. But in the end, the woman was hauled off, still bent in half like a hair pin.

"Who on earth was she?" gasped Enid as the crowd continued to press forward pushing her and her neighbour with it.

The fishwife, now somewhat at sixes and sevens as a result of her combative efforts, cast her a surprised glance: "Why, man, that's Miss Phillips, the new leader of the WSPU. Did ye not knaa that?'"

Enid blushed. But she didn't have time to respond because a uniformed elbow caught her hard on the side of her head, and she crumpled to her knees.

*

It was a bitter evening, and the gaslights flared like daggers along the street. Outside the Assembly Rooms, the crowd from the station had reformed and augmented itself and was fidgeting and manoeuvring uneasily. It had taken Enid several cups of sugary tea from the station cafeteria to gather her wits and to overcome the terrible throbbing in her temple. But now, here she was, in their midst, waiting for whatever might unfold. A dogged determination prevailed in most quarters but, here and there, a note of anger had been minted in the cold.

"Let the dog see the rabbit, wor Bobby!" yelled a woman in a squashed black hat. "We'll tell the bastard what's what."

"You'll clap eyes on him soon enough," a constable on duty replied, shoving her well back into the crowd.

The guests began to arrive, some in horse-drawn vehicles and others in motor cars. The horses, unsettled by the ruckus, snorted and blew out mighty cones of steam that almost touched the pavement. The motor cars coughed fumes from their exhausts. As each man ascended the steps into the hall, he adopted either a dismissive and stony-faced demeanour, or the casual air of a socialite attending a high-class ball. Still no sign of Churchill.

After a long wait in which feet went numb, and tonsils stiffened, a motor car finally slid up to the curb. Churchill! The women immediately began their agitation, their single, shouted demand filling the night air.

The doors of the vehicle swung open and Churchill emerged, one elegant boot, one slender trouser leg at a time, until there he was, at full height, in his winter coat with the recognisable Persian lamb collar, a bow tie visible at his throat, below the wingtips of his shirt. The crowd, unused to so much elegance, and resentful of it, increased their pushing and shoving.

Churchill took some moments to adjust his top hat to his satisfaction. The lips were full and sensual, the nostrils almost porcine, the gaze aloof. There was nothing here that deterred or intimidated him. He turned and was hustled, with as much dignity as his minions could muster, up the steps and into the hall. But there was something in the imperviousness of that gaze, that look of entitlement, that triggered outrage. The desire to wrest justice from him, to bend an unfair system into one that accommodated present needs, gave rise to pandemonium. The crowd surged forward, the police cordon broke, and that was when Enid's luck changed.

Along with a few others, she was swept up the steps, from where it seemed only logical that she should worm her way into the vestibule. After that, she had no problem squeezing between the elbows of gentlemen, up the grand staircase and into the gallery.

The crowd ranks in the auditorium settled. A hush fell, broken only by one or two bouts of coughing. Mr Churchill was welcomed to the podium by the president of the Liberal club. He gathered himself, fiddled with his watch chain, stuck a forefinger in his waistcoat pocket and began his speech. From outside the roar of the women could still be heard, occasionally amplified by a megaphone. He started on trade tariffs.

"Will women get the vote this session?" came a cry from the floor of the house. There was a kerfuffle while a woman in green gabardine was hustled out. He began on unemployment.

"Will votes for women be in the King's speech, Mr Churchill?" This time a voice from further back. More commotion, and another woman dispensed with, her hat rolling away among the feet of her neighbours as she was hauled off.

"I'd just like to point out," Churchill digressed, waving his hand in her general direction, "that if foolish women like these forget their sex, they leave no reason to complain if men sometimes do so, also." The audience murmured their approval. He now moved on to reform of the House of

Lords.

"No taxation without representation!" shrieked a woman standing near Enid. She, too, was made to disappear in a matter of moments. Enid scribbled frantically.

*

It was too late to get home, so she sat at a tram stop, the cold nibbling at her fingers, and drafted her report.

*

"My goodness!" said Hattie, settling herself at her desk first thing the following morning, and casting an eye over Enid's appearance. "What did you get up to last night?"

Mr. Peabody summoned them into his office. "Right, George, let's be havin' it."

"All there, Mr. Peabody." George slapped down an untidy sheaf of typing on to the desk.

"How did it go, then?"

"Champion. Nae bother. He said what he came to say. All about free trade an' that."

Enid looked at him in surprise. "You mean there were no disruptions?"

"None that I saw."

"You were there and you saw nothing?" Enid was scandalised. She put her own careful work down on the desk. "That's a full report, Mr. Peabody, right from the moment Mr Churchill set foot on the platform till the moment the meeting disbanded. Either George wasn't there, or he's got a very partial view."

Mr. Peabody stared at her for some time, the pin from the county cricket club winking dully in his tweedy lapel. The air hung heavy in the office.

"It's George's report, and that's what we'll be using," he pronounced eventually. Where's your piece on Chandernagore?"

"I haven't finished it."

"Why not?"

She didn't know where the words came from. No-one had ever taught her to swear.

"Calcutta is the arsehole of Empire, Mr. Peabody, and Chandernagore is twenty miles up it."

*

She crossed the bridge over the river and parked her bike against the wall of the cricket ground. Six months without paid work now, and her father's anger with her unabated. Still. If a job was worth doing… She hitched up her skirts and climbed up and over the stone wall. There, in front of her, the pitch and, even more invitingly, the wicket used by the club's first eleven. In the distance she heard the whoop of the mainline train as it thundered south towards the seat of government. She took the trowel from her pocket and struck it deep into the sweet, fleshy turf. She hummed a few bars of maestro Verdi's *Dies Irae* to herself as she set about her task. After twenty minutes, she sat back on her hunkers to admire her handiwork: 'Work before play, boys. Votes for women!'

Dharti Khoon aur Paani
Dipesh Pandya

human fights ignite for human rights
spiked metal roadblock borderlines
cash and burn farmland to war zone torsion
the government sleeps on a deathbed of nails
students—dadas—dadis and truth tellers jailed
sedition sedition listen the people have risen
riot gear tear gas tight assed heartless rss fakir
get the fuck outta here

tanks and tractors
land owners and land grabbers
fake facts and fat bankers
aam aadmi balm sound the alarm
at delhi's door no winter warmers
modi government enforces traumas
fascism doesn't need commas
fool stop. political dogmas
for years the people warned us
now they messing with the farmers
circle jerked by corporate piranhas
standing by idle will only harm us

tera jhuth hai bohot bhari
yeh patloon pathaani
sar pe lal tikka nahin khooni
phir bhi dil hai imandari

bhaarat shararat—izzat aur adalat
infiltrators and committee pirates
fists grow from hands that sow
prostrate—protest—protect
the divide is wide minus our lands
sad addition—edition sedition repetition
garam—a garam fried fascism
multiply shaheen bagh mission
don't fuss—just trust us
people equal regal sequels

32

prime time sinister your time will come
swift karma tractorvism continuum

oye modi
kis haal mein hai kisan
o teri , o teri o
betaab hai tera hisaab
kis haal mein hai kisan
o teri , o teri o
yahaan lathi
wahaan bhi lathi
lathi yahaan
lathi wahaan
har maang pe hai naka bandhi
har jawab ka khoon aur paani
oye modi
kis haal mein hai kisan
o teri , o teri o

In the Slips
Pratibha Castle

While the world watches
Violetta, clad in years
the measure of a week,
journeys from Odessa
with her doll and cat

and a Grandma
her face a crumpled map
of lifetime drills
framed by a scarf
the colour of losing
urges a boy soldier
put this flower in your pocket

hopes his flesh
rotted into trampled mud
bone and blood
transmuted to
a claggy womb
will birth a crop
of smiling sunflowers

and men in black,
as if spectators
at a cricket match,
watch a tank
grizzle over cobblestones
across the city square
while a man
sprints into its path
scoops up a hand-grenade
underarms it
at a pile of rubble
the dog-end
dangling from his lip
a red-eyed fuse

Poem for Workers' Memorial Day
Anne Caldwell

Grace Newell, great grandmother, cotton weaver,
Herbert Clarke, great grandfather, cotton sizer.
My family were Tod mill-workers, signing
to each other, deaf from the looms' clatter.

At the same time, seven Wainstall Waifs were
buried in Luddenden Dene. Child labourers
who worked a regulated nine-and-half-hour day;
a 56-hour week. Aged eleven.

Those nimble, Liverpool girls yearned
for their mothers and salt-blown city,
on their hands and knees—under the oily
machines of weaving sheds.

Half a century on, a woman never understood
the danger of Acre Mill. Gently washed
her husband's overalls with carbolic love.
Contracted cancer from the dust.

Eight members of the foreman's
family (all with scarred lungs) hugged
their father, covered in white powder,
a time-bomb blooming in his chest.

Their neighbour was up on the rim
of the moors when his tractor tipped
over. He listened to the curlews and cried
for help. A limb crushed.

There's a snowdrop garden planted
with care at Pecket Well, a modest plaque
and contemplation bench; a lethal dump
is capped; our woods singing with wrens.

Today, we've learnt to love the understated
beauty of a stone rill that took water from
reservoir to mill. Wainsgate alive with the promise
of wood anemones and astrantia.

We remember the loved, the rubbed-out.
Shoulder to shoulder with bus drivers, shop workers,
hospital porters, Covid coursing through
the world's lungs. The rubbed-out.

Hybrid orchids bloom each year
where Acre Mill once stood.
Purple trumpets of hope
dotted in tussock grass and heather.

Haft Tapeh Workers' Demo
Nasrin Parvaz

The Kiss
Nasrin Parvaz

Women's Demonstration
Nasrin Parvaz

Can You Guess What It Is Yet?
K Searle

Chicken shop, betting shop, pound store,
Coffee shop, betting shop, pound store,
Coffee shop, whole foods shop, pound store,
Coffee shop, whole foods shop, realtor.

G E _ T _ _ F _ C _ T _ _ _

Answer:

41

Make Your Own Protest Sticker
K Searle

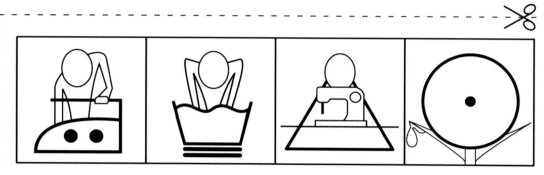

MADE IN BABYLON
(100% OPPRESSED LABOUR)

Antigone
Claire HM

Sister   are you saying   you won't
help honour   our lion of a brother
as he lies   determined   in his death?

If that's so   then   if you sense
we've suffered   enough,   think on.
If you're   dutiful   to the state

that says   our brother   must keep paying
even after   death   that he'll be
    unburied   un-mourned   dry

of tears because you fear   the penalty
of a heartless state   do not call yourself   sister.
I'd   bury him   if I   had strength,

crack open   the rigid   world
he lies on,   where you'd   let him rot.
Instead   I'll use the means   I have

cover him   in ritual   in the finest
    layer of dust   rustle
    at the edges   where open mouthed

    caves wait   to gulp me   down
when I refuse   what is legal   and cruel
    to pick   instead
    what's unlawful
    and just.

What will it take for a British Revolution?
Sarah O'Connor

You raise an eyebrow when I suggest your stiff
upper lip may be a precursor to rigor mortis.
For didn't you get your Magna Carta
in 1215 and wasn't that enough?
A polite march has a place perhaps,
but as that breaks Hancock's rule of six…

Better not dear, better not.

Somewhere
a rash young boy
        begs
                Can they have some more?
as those who claim to represent us
vote to sell Bevan family jewels
to foreign cash buyers.

Surely not dear. Surely not.

we sit transfixed by rising graphs//watching no.66//kill Granny with a coffee
on his walk//swallow whole their medicine of misinformation//as these
returned Viceroys//lord it over their new locals//starved of scrutiny//we
camouflage our self-harm scars.

Their headlines shout warnings of Communist
solidarity, 'til you can't see this great eagle's head
for what it is. Your fascists wear comic book costumes—
not pencil skirts, pearls, and a dead-eyed stare.

Plague gives us something simple to count//but how many deaths in a decade
caused by want//or fear of deportation to a pretty camp//running water is a
luxury these days.

There are more ways
of killing a cat
than guns
and gas
and a forced labour march.

Never mind dear. Never mind.

Walking from the Station
Sarah O'Connor

after W.B.Yeats

I

This is no city for lone women. Night
brings chill breaths of bogeymen
made flesh and uniform. No saviour
of safe passage awaits in this valley
of tears. A pregnant friend may ask
for your hat to piss in—she just
hopes golden showers don't appear
in your search history.

II

You are the rotten fruit,
but I am the apple core—
chewed up; seed-spat;
nothing but a pair of tits.
As your sap hardens into
putrid rind of brute reality,
I fail to flag down
the 198 to Themyscira.

III

So tell me who to call on now—
Athene's spear or her wise owl? Hera's
protective wedding vows? Protected who?
Not Persephone, Alcmena, Callisto,
Nemesis. Not Cassiopeia or Leda—
to name just Zeus' rapes. Is it normal
to know which of my photos I hope
they'll use in the Daily Mail?

IV

What self defence class could help
this marble block of hammered flesh,
crushed hope and fear-soured breath?
No keys dug between my knuckles
can halt your birthright to stop and search,
a silenced bird, who should have known
what did; and was; and always is;
coming for her.

Jenny Geddes in St Giles[2]
A C Clarke

Thwack! The faldstool flying through the air
catches the Minister off-balance.
Does he think the goodwives of Canongate
will take his Romish service sitting down?

Jenny's first up, foulmouthing him and his flock,
her market trader's voice has bawled out a wheen
of diddlers. Woe worth the day that any chiel
should try to cozen her out of her due!

Hannay's no better, spite of his priest's gown.
In seconds it's raining stools, stones, even Bibles
as if the word of God could strike the blaspheme
out of his mouth. The noise! It summons up

the officers. Shoved out, the hecklers pound
the bolted door—why should the king's minions
defile their worship? Bad cess to them!
No crying quits for Jenny and her fellows.

To arms!

---

2   *On 23 July 1637 Jenny Geddes, a market-trader in Edinburgh, hurled a faldstool (folding stool) at the officiating minister in St Giles, James Hannay. This action is credited with initiating a series of riots in the city against the imposition of the Book of Common Prayer on the Presbyterian Church of Scotland (which associated it and Anglican liturgies with Roman Catholic practices).*

Those who wait
Rod Whitworth

After Anna Kamienska

Those who sit against the supermarket wall
the bank   the coffee bar
and ask for change.
Those who queue
for a foodbank parcel
for a brief slot
on a library computer.
Those who wait
for camp days to end
for return to the homeland.
Those whose time
is circumscribed by bars
cemented there by injustice.
Those who wonder
when it all will end.
May they all find their homeland
like a migrating swallow   like my neighbour's pigeons
like a compass needle finding north   water finding its level.

May they all find their homeland.

House of Cards
Rod Whitworth

Snip.
This peerage
is cheap
at twice
the price.

Snap
my fingers
and PMs come running
to give me ermine.

Snorum
and yawnum.
We are our lordships
with titles to sloth.

High-cock-a-lorum.
We strut and we preen,
Lord Never-Was, Lady Has-Been.

"They Did Not Realize We Are Human Beings"
Jess Skyleson

-Maitha Jolet, a 61-year-old Marshallese who was one of the first to move to Dubuque,
Iowa, after the U.S. dropped nuclear bombs on their Pacific Island home

Much easier to think it was God's ink-stained hands
who signed that bargain, that it was his lips
blowing dry the words
on a promise that was never made
to a people
he did not intend to keep—

They did not realize
we are human beings.

How clean to blast islands from the map,
they leave behind no tell-tale mark, no jagged cliffs
of excised limbs, nothing but the name
of a swimsuit, famous for what is missing
and the craters
of belly-buttons, visible in tender flesh—

They did not realize
we are human beings.

The distance far enough that the clouds
of glowing ash could be imagined
as the outline of a movie-monster,
all foam and makeup made to disguise
grotesque shapes
growing in a motherless womb—

They did not realize
we are human beings.

And so perhaps they thought no one would notice,
that we would choose not to see

the feathers of these birds of paradise,
wings broken and nests torn down,
perching unsteadily
in the shade of Iowa's cornfields—

But they did not realize
we are human beings.

The Scoville Scale - A Clavis On Protest
Electra Rhodes

The Scoville Scale? A measurement of pungency, a cataloguing of spice. An equation that calculates the heat by which we might measure our lives. Where the intervals are logarithmic, doubling each time. A quick escalation from cool to impossible. To something unbearable. Fast.

Where the first level is 0 - 700, non-pungent and barely noticeable. The mildest occasions of both living and loving. Where every uniform you meet will protect your best interests. And you know there is an equal opportunity 'we' that 'they' are there to serve.

Where the second level is 700 - 3,000, mildly pungent, a background hint of something. A thrill or a frisson. Even a little spice to your day, when you see someone stopped in the street. And the soon-to-be criminal waves their arms wildly so you reluctantly conclude that their arrest makes total sense.

Where the third level is 3,000 - 25,000, moderately pungent. And that's noticeable. Flavouring different parts of your day. And though it is worse for other people, sweat pools in the tender places of your body. In the tender places of your life. Heat is coming for you and you can't get out the way.

Where the fourth level is 25,000 - 70,000, highly pungent. And that's suffocating and inescapable on every kettled corner. And though you search for some way out, there is no equivocation. And you realise that it's too late to beg for quenching, because they hope that you will burn.

Where the fifth level is above 80,000, very highly pungent. And your breath comes short and ragged. And you're scared that this might be dry drowning. Where each part of you is scrutinised on the front page of every paper. And you see yourself consumed a million times in other people's eyes.

Where official Law Enforcement Pepper Spray is measured at 1,500,000 - 3,000,000 Scoville Units. And it is an obliteration. Of you, your self, your every aspiration. Of everyone in the vicinity and more. More. More. Where a blast across the face tells you there is no 'we' in 'us' and you are, as you have always been, a mere obstacle on the front line. And your small protest and resistance is extinguishable, futile, and incandescently feared.

The Ousterbout
Electra Rhodes

The day is spike-sprackled and winter-glorious, the neighbours are primed, and Gran is squawking fit to burst her way out of the prison of the bailiff's arms. He is new. Worried by the gutterings of the charm-sparse audience.

Every quarter the landlord lickspittles his rent book and sends an ousterbout bailiff after the cash or put by.

The bailiff is a big man. Slabbed. With a face like two sides of meat. The sort of chump chops you dream of not sharing for your dinner. Tasty, with a side of spuds and peas.

He'll take what he can. A pair of shoes. A coat. A coal scuttle. Brass for preference. Anything he can hawk or scrap or get a bit of pawn for.

Today there are six vans who've not turned their shillings in for the last three months. The landlord wants them gone.

The first van houses a lass, three barefoot children at her side and a baby buried in her arms. They are silent, already coffined. As the audience hisses, the bailiff veers away from them, fast.

The second van is up on blocks and shuttered. Even he has the sense to see there is no point in a hammered ask at the padlocked door.

At the third van he reckons Gran will be easy pickings. Now, she's kicking through his shins and screeching like the factory whistle half the camp tout for.

Someone calls a copper and, though they'd not usually come into the camp, this one has an uneasy 'now then' with the family. He snaps a look at the bailiff holding Gran off the ground, then shakes his head dolly-lagging ragged. She ends up in a crumpled, hollering heap of foul-feckle fury.

The bailiff and the copper have nose to nose words while the audience rumbles and rises, a barometer threatening an imminent storm. There is a quick fumble of coins, the metal glinting in the watery sunshine. A wee flash of un-summer lightning ready to ignite the eked out fumes of the hour.

The copper hands Gran her compensation for the mishandling. Meek as a doorstep cadge, Gran gathers herself and hands the bailiff his own coins. He gawps at the money in his outstretched palm, then up and back at her. She scrawls her way to full height, all five foot two in her patched button boots and scratched up bun. And then brittle-sticks out her other hand, ready for the sixpence in change he now owes her.

The audience laughs. Big poverty-bowl bellies and red chap-rashed faces. The bailiff glances around. He's been got good and he knows it. He hands over the money and she snaffles it away. He doesn't bother with the rest of the collectings. He knows he is done and dusted for the evening.

He does what he can for his leaking pride, sticking his chin in the air and bully beefing his shoulders through the crowd. Gran tooth gaps a grin, handing the copper half a ready sixpence from her pocket. Weren't only the neighbours who were trimmed and primed ready for this day.

1990
Caitlin Kendall

That was the summer you turned seven and the tar bubbled up
from the roads. Your dad showed you how to fry an egg
on the bonnet of your brown Volvo estate car.
The winter before, you had stood, barefoot
on the floorboards of your living room and watched
the Berlin wall come down on your 12" TV screen.
You can still see those images when you close your eyes.

That was the summer that the air crackled with change
so hot your mum brought cold flannels when she came
to pick you up from school and talked to you
about Greenhouse gases and the Ozone layer.

That was the summer Mum bought you an ice-cream
in the park everyday after school: 99s from Mr Curley-top,
a white whirl resting on its wafer cone, dripping
in monkey's blood; its chocolate flake a unicorn horn.
Back then they really did cost 99p.

That was the summer that Maggie Thatcher resigned
and your mum bought you TWO ice-creams.
You were sticky with happiness, your hand speckled with flaked metallic
paint from the playground, the small gravel stones
of springy tarmac between your fingers.

That was the summer you went to a party, waving a paper South Africa flag:
your parents told you that a man named Nelson Mandela was finally free.
You stood in the darkened community centre and watched
the projected wrinkled images from half the world away
as the whole world unfurled before you.

labrador gives post-election press conference
Hilary Watson

on behalf of all dogs at polling stations, humans, thank you so much for giving us your vote. sorry for weeing under the podium just now, i'm just so excited. we, that's all good dogs, are so happy we got to vote for you. good dogs can sense good people. & you started saying why don't we just give dogs the vote! i knew we could fix your problem with the e-ewe & breakfast. we loved your candidate lists, great people. i don't need to tell you that some of our favourite people are humans. we didn't need your lists (we couldn't actually read them). anyway, we voted for the best trees instead. oh & the whales. i know you know whales are the trees of the sea & trees full stop are so wise. trees don't need to sit in wetmincestir because—you probably didn't realise this—palaces are made of dead trees. it's okay! no one is mad. an honest mistake. you're in such good hands. trees & whales have the best hands. they'll take care of everything. we can go home for walkies & dinner! (i love that word so much) so thank you, we had such a good time. here's my selfie smile! oh, almost forgot… any questions?

Choices
JP Seabright

Throw yourself into the street my love,
defend your home with fists and knives,
your children with guns and lives.

Mother is making Molotovs at midnight,
a recipe handed down in the family
from grandma who told stories of democracy.

How in times gone by there were choices,
you'd elect a party to make decisions for all,
now ten green bottles stand on our wall.

The only parties are where someone has died,
when we gather in darkness to celebrate a life
and risk lighting candles to honour their light.

The only choice is whether to run or fight,
when barriers are built to repel neighbours,
still we imagine someone else will save us.

So prepare your weapons of kitchen utensils,
plan your escape route or choose your death,
singing songs of peace under your breath:

Wipe the blood from the soil,
clear the earth, make a hole,
and there, in the dirt, plant a sunflower.

Balloon to China
Craig Aitchison

Was someone crying? Ryan hesitated before taking the final couple of steps to the door. No. Just the sound of someone talking, he reassured himself, then tapped on the door before nudging it open. A woman looked up from placing clothes into a bag, nodded, then returned to her task, talking to herself, checking the items as she put them neatly away.

Ryan looked at the list of names and destinations on his clipboard. There were no details to say how long they'd waited to hear that they were to be sent home, no reasons why they couldn't stay, no story about why they'd sought asylum in the UK. When Ryan heard that phrase—asylum seekers— he thought of Hide and Seek, like it was some sinister game, like safety was somewhere if you just looked hard enough. Not for these people though. Their time was up.

Just do the job, he reminded himself. Check the list. Mae Margai. To be returned to Sierra Leone via Cameroon. There should be a son too. Ryan t leaned into the room, scanning for the boy. He wasn't there.

Then, from behind, he heard the clatter of feet and he looked down at a small boy clutching a football. The boy, Siaka Margai, nudged past him into the room.

His mother looked the boy up and down, frowning, as if considering whether to scold him for the muck on his trousers and trainers, before handing the boy a holdall. He tucked the ball under his arm, put the bag over his shoulder and joined Ryan at the door.

The woman was opening drawers. She must be checking she had everything. Not that they'd have much. He stayed in the corridor, not wanting to intrude.

The boy stood next to him. He was just a kid, his smile open and friendly, even though Ryan was there to take him away.

"You like football?" Ryan said.

The boy's eyes widened. "I love football. I like many English players - Raheem Sterling, Harry Kane, Marcus Rashford. But I love Mbappe best. In my village my friend call me Mbappe. I score goals like him."

"Okay. I'll call you Mbappe too."

The boy pouted his lips and folded his arms in a trademark Mbappe goal celebration, so that the ball fell from his grasp and rolled along the floor. He ran after it, like a little Mbappe, chasing a through ball. Ryan leaned back into the room. "We leave in five minutes," he said and walked out, along the corridor, past grey doors to the only one that stood open. Ryan flicked through the documents, checking the details: Sadio Kpundeh. Inside, a tall man was folding a shirt neatly and placing it into a black holdall.

"I am ready," the man announced.

Ryan nodded. Then he saw Geoff, the senior escort, walking towards them. Better follow orders. Better do it right.

Ryan took some handcuffs from his belt and held them towards Sadio. "They will not be necessary."

"Just a precaution, you know. We have to do it." Ryan said and he clipped them around Sadio's wrists, trying to keep them loose.

Geoff came to the door, nodded, and he and Sadio followed Geoff to the reception area. Geoff stopped to collect papers; the young woman behind the desk turned away.

They stepped out into the drizzle. Geoff turned to Sadio. "See, it's not all bad. You'll not get this back in your own country," he said then slid the door of the people carrier open. Ryan and Geoff got in the back. The driver— Geoff didn't know his name—didn't even turn around before driving off.

The drive to Heathrow stuttered. Ryan alternated between flicking through the paper and staring blankly out of the window at traffic cones and drizzle. As they neared the airport he noticed more planes, landing and taking off. In three and a half weeks it would be him, two weeks in Tenerife, just him and Kate. He imagined her nudging him in the ribs and telling him to listen to the stewardess. "You never know," she'd say. "And anyway, she's just doing her job." Kate was right, the smile, make-up, instructions that no-one listened to: it was her job.

"Nearly there," he said to Geoff.

As he did so, the van squeaked to a halt again. He picked up the paper, turning to an inside page with a bold title: 'Evicted'. A picture of a blonde model in a bikini dominated the page.

"You don't watch that crap do you?" said Geoff, leaning over.

"I won't now, if she's out," Ryan replied, flicking over. "You?"

"The wife does. I see bits."

On the next page there was another full colour picture, this time a girl of five or six in a blue cardigan holding a pink balloon.

"Listen to this Geoff: 'A helium balloon released at a school fête on a rainy day in Cheshire has been found in southern China.'" He paused, then summarised. "This little girl let this balloon go in Chester; eight weeks later some bloke in China found it and sent back a note. 'Meteorologists are baffled' apparently. There's a map." He stabbed a finger at the crude image. "Carried by a jet stream, they reckon."

Geoff leaned over from the seat behind and beside him, in the aisle, Sadio turned. "That's a bloody long way," Geoff said.

"6,000 miles."

"Like I said. A bloody long way." Geoff paused. "I got my girl a balloon the other week. Hold onto it, I said. It was a dog, a Dalmatian. We were walking through the park, hand in hand, and suddenly she stopped. Didn't say a word, just squeezed my hand tighter and looked up. So did I. There it was floating away, up and up. We just stood there and watched it, not speaking. It wasn't until it went out of sight that she suddenly started crying. Wouldn't stop till I got her an ice-cream. Maybe it's in China too."

"Maybe."

And then it was quiet. Geoff leaned back in his chair; Ryan turned to the football pages; Sadio smiled a tiny smile. The car started moving again, picking up speed, the water droplets on the windows no longer falling vertically, but being dragged back horizontally.

Mbappe had fallen asleep soon after getting into the car. Mae closed her eyes and slept too. The motion seemed to stir Mbappe; he shuffled and blinked into wakefulness. He pushed himself forwards, then became gradually aware of the seat belt holding him down. It was too high and had made a mark on the side of his face. He held a hand to his crotch and leaned over to Ryan:

"I need to pee."

"Soon. We're nearly there."

"Where? Where are we going?"

"The airport. You're going in a big plane. Just like that one." Ryan pointed out of the window where a plane seemed to struggle into the air, as if it was held to the ground or pushed down by the weight of drizzle and darkness. Mbappe kept looking at Ryan.

"Where to?"

Ryan kept watching the plane over Mbappe's shoulder.

"Tell him," Sadio said. He looked directly at Ryan, his voice loud in the van. "Tell him where we are going. Tell him you are sending him home to a country at war. A country where he is not safe. A country he and his mother left in fear, to seek refuge in this fine nation. But where he is not welcome. Tell him."

"OK mate, that's enough," said Geoff, but Sadio did not stop.

"Why can't you tell him that he is not welcome in this country? This country he has dreamed of when he sees your football. Do you even know where you are sending him? What you are sending him to?"

Geoff unbuckled his seatbelt. "Stop this."

Sadio kept speaking. "He's a child. A child."

Geoff grabbed Sadio's arm. "Shut up. You're upsetting the boy."

Ryan got to his feet, crouching unsteadily as the car sped forward. "It's OK. Geoff, sit down." He placed a hand on Geoff's chest, until his body relaxed and slumped back into his seat.

Sadio glanced across at Mbappe whose face was pressed to his mother's shoulder. Mae stroked her son's hair but stared straight ahead. Sadio spoke again, softly, "I am sorry." He stared directly into Ryan's eyes and Ryan returned the look, seeing the red veins in his eyes. He turned back to Geoff, who sat with his arms taut, blood under his skin rushing, making patches on his arms stand out where laser surgery had nearly removed tattoos.

"You OK?" asked Ryan.

"Fine."

"Nearly there."

And then, as Ryan turned to face the front, another voice: "I need to pee," pleaded Mbappe.

There was silence for the rest of the journey. Ryan looked out the window. The rain stopped. A slight 'Humph' from Geoff when he saw a sign protesting against the building of a new runway was the only sound. The traffic was no longer a problem and Geoff knew the security guards. He did this run every week and seemed to be able to flash a piece of paper and nod his head backwards to make barriers rise. When they arrived at Terminal Four he walked around and opened the door. Sadio stepped out, holding his cuffed hands out.

Entering the terminal, two men and a woman in high-visibility jackets and a policeman with a gun slung over his shoulder acknowledged them. They were led through the departure lounge. They cut through people who were chatting, shopping, drinking; anything to fill this in-between time. They went through a door and down stairs until they ended up in a room which seemed more dimly lit, quieter, away from the bustle of the public areas. Ryan looked up to see a small departure board: KQ101, departure 9am. On time. Almost done, get them on the plane and get away. Ryan wondered if he would sleep when he got home.

One of the airport staff led them into a small, empty departure lounge, then walked off with Geoff, as Ryan called out: "Milk, two sugars. And strong."

A cleaner came in, emptied a bin and left again. Geoff returned with the coffees.

Mbappe began to tug on his mother's dress, again holding his crotch.

Ryan stood up, "I'll take him." He held out his hand in a gesture to Mbappe to follow him but was surprised when Mbappe took his hand and began to pull him towards the toilet. It was dark when they entered but an automatic switch tripped and lights flickered and then dazzled them. Ahead of Ryan were sinks and he was confronted by himself in the mirror, pale and bloodshot. He would sleep when he got home.

He walked to the sink and pushed the cold tap, water spluttering into his cupped hands, which he splashed onto his face. He placed his hands under the tap again but already the flow had stopped. He pushed it again, but then became aware of a tugging on his trouser leg. He looked down at Mbappe bouncing on his tiptoes, then at the urinals. They were all too high. He couldn't reach.

"Christ." Wiping his hands on his trousers, he followed Mbappe towards them.

Mbappe unzipped his trousers and pulled down his pants and stretched out his arms. He put his hands under Mbappe's armpits and lifted him, holding him steady and looking away as he heard a trickle.

"Finish," said Mbappe.

Ryan put him down. Mbappe fastened his trousers and walked to the sink, again looking helplessly towards Ryan.

"Leave them. They'll be fine," Ryan said, walking out of the toilet.

Mae gathered Mbappe into her legs as they walked back into the departure lounge, holding his head and whispering into his ear.
Geoff got up and walked to a vending machine:"Give me a minute."

Ryan sat down next to Sadio, who was sitting with his head bowed and cuffed hands in his lap, as if in prayer. He said something, Ryan straining to hear, "Pardon?"

"I am sorry. For my behaviour before. It was wrong." He lifted his head and turned to look at Ryan, "You are not at fault, you are simply doing the bidding of your government."

Ryan looked away to the vending machine which Geoff was thumping and replied, "You don't have to apologise."

"I have accepted my fate. I have spent almost a year in that place, like a prison, trying to appeal to lawyers and diplomats and now I will return to my country. It is likely that I will die there. I have come to accept that. But the boy…"

Geoff had returned and sat across from Sadio and Ryan. His can fizzed as he popped the ring-pull. He sipped the Coke from the top of the can but kept his eyes on Sadio. Near-silence settled, Ryan becoming aware of the muffled activity of the airport.

Then a member of airport staff walked in. He passed a high-visibility jacket to Geoff, threw another towards Ryan. "They can board. We get them on the plane and get home."

"Thank God," replied Ryan.

The doors slid open and they stepped outside. After the clinical gleam of the building it was good to be on ground level, looking up at the bulk of the planes. The bulbous nose-cone of the plane was in front, further off there were various trucks, hump-backed, awkward-looking with bright chevrons tattooed across them. Lights reflected in puddles.

Keeping within the painted lines, they walked towards the plane. At first the air was cold, but a warmth washed over them, and with it, the smell of fumes. Ryan stayed at the rear, just behind Mbappe who was holding his mother's hand. Mbappe's head moved from side to side, taking in the movement of machines all around. It should be exciting, Ryan thought. A little boy's paradise.

The last passengers were walking up the metal stairs to board the plane, stewardesses smiling at them as they entered, people holding suitcases, handbags and newspapers, taking holidays, visiting families, returning home. Geoff was first to the top of the stairs and bent down to speak in the ear of the stewardess. She stepped away. Sadio ducked his head slightly as he entered and Ryan spoke while unlocking the cuffs. "Officials will be waiting for you in Cameroon. They will escort you to your connecting flight."

Sadio followed a steward down the aisle. Ryan felt a tug on his trouser leg and heard a voice say "Goodbye."

"Goodbye, Mbappe."

"Look for me. When I play for PSG. I will win Champions League, World Cup."

"I hope so."

"Of course. Remember Mbappe."

"I will."

And then they were gone, Mae taking his hand and leading him to his seat. Ryan watched Mbappe fumble with his seabelt until his mother reached across and secured it. Then Ryan turned and walked down the stairs and away from the plane without looking back. He didn't want to see the plane taxi away or lift into the air. He didn't wait for Geoff to catch up with him, just walked back towards the automatic doors of the terminal.

He needed to get back to the car and get away. He needed to go home.

wear black, bring flowers
Deborah Finding

wear black, bring flowers
we have so many vigils now
that we've started to introduce dress codes
just to mix it up
Sarah. Sabina. Ashling.
don't worry if you forget these names
dead women are like buses
except you don't wait for ages
and then three come along at once

what are you expecting this will achieve?
he asks, as he watches me
cutting out my circle of cardboard
from the most recent Amazon box, expertly
piercing a star in the centre
to hold my candle
already half-burned from the one before

nothing, I reply,
as I check my funeral-casual look in the mirror,
and pick up the supermarket bunch of red carnations I bought earlier
in anticipation of laying them down uselessly
when I get there, along with the others
a sea of colourful tributes
on the ground, covered in plastic, waiting to rot in the rain
nothing. obviously, absolutely nothing.
I'm not naïve. I'm not stupid.

yes we got that message through our thick skulls
whether the knowledge was delivered
that time we weren't believed
or that other time we were advised not to make a fuss
or in that moment we realised the police weren't there to protect us that day
or on that day that bill didn't pass and that MP made a joke about it
or simply when we internalised the expectation
that we will continue to set light to candles, but not petrol
and that our fists will always be too full of flowers to fight

we know our screams are silenced by the soft pillow over our faces
we know our tears serve no purpose
other than for the photographer to get his shot
so he can leave this crowd of women and go home early
we know.
we know.
but we go anyway
because we also know
that not going feels
a little bit worse

Gatekeepers
Lara Frankena

Helmeted, booted, beetled by body armour,
three soldiers breaking through a metal gate

are confronted in the courtyard by an old man
in knitted jumper and old woman in pink cap.

Empty-handed, they approach despite
warning shot, scolding in a common tongue:

How dare you? Have you no shame?
The intruders retreat from this barrage of words.

Gun barrels droop, tip downwards as the couple
march the soldiers back through the gate,

a little dog swirling at their feet.

Exposé
Dipika Mummery

Send or delete?

Amit stares at the screen, hoping an answer will somehow present itself to him, here in his mouldy East London bedsit on a drizzly Tuesday evening.

Send or delete?

His stomach growls under his thin, creased shirt and he thinks of the dinner he has to look forward to: a potato that he will obliterate in the microwave before drowning it in cheap chilli sauce.

Better not think about the food being served back home, up north: the soft rotis, spiced meatballs, dal thick with ghee and cumin. Hot green chillies on top. Rice pudding for dessert. All paid for from what he sent home, like the years when his parents sent their wages back to India. Except that his pounds don't have to cross any borders to reach their destination.

Send or delete?

The email came at lunchtime. The sender—one of the managers cocooned in their cosy little offices—seemed not to have realised that she'd sent it to the wrong person. He read all two lines of the email several times to see who it was intended for, but found nothing, so he opened the attachment. The urgent red text at the top of each page made him think of the bills his mother used to receive not long after his father died, before he found this job. Memories of hunger, cold, a joyless house.

Send or delete?

All of the managers were in a meeting. He did it without thinking: a USB drive hanging from his key ring went into his computer, and he copied the file across, his heart drumming fast and his palms suddenly cold yet damp. He knew how to completely delete the email, remove all trace of the fact that it had ever got to him at all, hide the file transfer.

He knew why he did all of these things.

Send or delete?

Back at the bedsit, he read the words. Struggled to understand. And then, suddenly, clarity. And an idea.

A dull ache started in his chest.

Who would lose their job from a leak this close to a general election? Heads would roll, but not the right ones. They were only a consultancy, not civil service.

Still, the implications. The headlines. The horror. They would sniff him out, despite all the precautions he took.

They would obliterate him.

Send or delete?

They know what they're doing. No one hoodwinked them, not like he'd been hoodwinked. They know exactly where this data came from. What it's for. Who will benefit.

Who will benefit? Not Amit, that's for sure. Certainly not his mother, smelling of oil and chillies, feet up in front of the television after a day of caring for Amit's sister, Indian drama blaring, eyelids sagging to a close. Not his neighbours, who drag themselves to and from the food bank each week, their shoulders hunched just a little bit more each time.
If he loses his job, that's it. Back home with his tail between his skinny legs, back to bills with red numbers on them. Back to his mother looking at him in consternation, wondering how she ended up with such a failure of a son. All he had to do was go to London, get a decent job, provide for her. Provide for his sister, who had spent the last two years bedridden, unable to work and earn.

Send or delete?

But how many red-lettered envelopes could he prevent by hitting 'send'? Because there'd be an uproar. Wouldn't there? Surely something would have to happen if everyone knew. If everyone realised that the government was planning to pull the ultimate swindle of the public purse— move all that money away from the people who needed it the most to the ones who had more than enough.

Send or delete?

If he didn't press send, all that would happen was the same old thing to the same old people. The same old things that outraged the privileged folks on the left for a moment before they went back to worrying about their own lives.

Send or delete?

He would just have to make sure he was never discovered. Disappear somewhere. Leave nothing behind.

Send or delete?

He's always wanted to go to the Highlands. Why not?

Send or...?

The Prisoners in Cell Block K
K.T. Slattery

Are not allowed out. They have fallen short of the Key master's standards.
K1—ate more than she should have. Her grandmother always told her fat
women deserve no friends. Others do not want to look at, let alone talk,
to them. They deserve to be alone—and so K1 is locked up for crimes against
consumerism. Fed intravenously once a day in hopes that she will forget how
to chew.

K2 did not do her homework, and subsequently, fell short of her potential.
Smart, but easily distracted. Instead of going to graduate school, she flew off
the handle and became, of all things, an air hostess.

K3 did not tidy her room. Her bed went unmade for weeks on end—overall,
she could be described as a dishevelled mess. Once she made a list—and then
forgot to bring it with her. Never ironed her sheets like her grandmother
taught her, nor scrubbed her floors with a toothbrush. She has been fitted with
a shock collar, like the animal she is until she learns that cleanliness is next to
godliness.

K4 is a lifer—an escape artist with a proclivity for self-expression; she has
incited rebellious behaviour in fellow inmates. The biggest threat to the
regime, she has been subdued by tranquilizers combined with Netflix and
social media immersion therapy. Has been fitted with a tracking device and
will remain in isolation until loneliness makes her malleable.

K5 was recently released on good behaviour. As long as she keeps up her
smiling façade and tows the Conformist party line, she shall be allowed her
freedom. Fitted with an earpiece, so her probation officer can guide her in the
modern quest for perfection in all aspects of life.

Author Biographies

1. **K.T. Slattery** is a West of Ireland based writer, originally from Memphis, Tennessee. Her poetry has appeared in *Ropes Literary Journal, The Blue Nib, Streetcake, Planet in Peril Anthology, Impspired, Trasna, Nightingale and Sparrow, Drawn to the Light,* and *Anti Heroin Chic.* She received a special mention in the 2020 Desmond O'Grady Poetry Competition, was a featured reader for Over the Edge in January 2021 and a featured writer in Trasna Literary Arts in February of the same year. In 2022 she was nominated for Galway's Cuirt Festival Over the Edge New Writer of the Year and is one of the featured writers in the collective, Pushed Toward the Blue Hour. When not writing, she can be found throwing the ball for her dogs or painting.

2. **K Searle**'s poetry and doodles explore a range of lived experiences, and often attempt to frame them within the broader social structures, and entangled histories which give them rise. Employing a dynamic variety of forms, from riddles to innovative visual poems, his work explores, among other themes, how 'race' and class intersect in our lives in late capitalism.

3. **Dipika Mummery** has recently completed the MA Creative Writing course at The University of Manchester. Her short fiction has been published in print and online by Comma Press, Arachne Press, Tasavvur and Fox & Windmill. She is currently working on her first novel. Dipika lives in Manchester, UK.

4. **Lara Frankena**'s poems have appeared in publications such as *Poetry News, Ink Sweat & Tears* and *Butcher's Dog* and were longlisted for the 2021 and 2022 Erbacce Prize. She lives in London.

5. **Deborah Finding** (she/her) is a queer feminist writer from the UK with a background in academia and activism. Her poems have been recently published in fourteen poems, The Friday Poem, Ink Drinkers Poetry and Hearth & Coffin. Her features and interviews have been published widely (including The Guardian, Huffington Post, DIVA magazine, IB Tauris and Routledge). She writes mainly on popular culture and human rights (with a particular focus on sexual and domestic violence), and holds a PhD on this topic from LSE's Gender Institute. Deborah has worked in several UK NGOs focusing on mental health and sexual violence, and remains passionate about these issues, as well as about the power of the arts in therapy. Originally from the North-East of England, Deborah now lives in London.

6. **Craig Aitchison** has an MLitt in Creative Writing from Stirling University. His writing in Scots has been shortlisted for the Wigtown Poetry Prize and this year he won both first and second prize in the Scots Language Short Story competition. He has had fiction published by *Crowvus Press, Fictive Dream, Northwords Now, Southlight, Pushing Out the Boat* and *Wyldblood*. In 2021 he was one of the poets commissioned by the Scottish Poetry Library to write a poem to commemorate 250 years of Sir Walter Scott. In 2022 his work will feature in Poetry Scotland and New Writing Scotland.

7. **JP Seabright** (she/they) is a queer writer living in London. They have three pamphlets published: Fragments from Before the Fall: An Anthology of Post-Anthropocene Poetry by Beir Bua Press; the erotic memoir NO HOLDS BARRED by Lupercalia Press, and GenderFux, a collaborative poetry pamphlet, by Nine Pens Press. MACHINATIONS, an experimental collaborative work is out in 2022 from Trickhouse Press, as is Be∞Cause, a microchap, from Ghost City Press. More of their work can be found at https://jpseabright.com and via Twitter @errormessage.

8. **Hilary Watson** is a poet from South Wales. She studied at the University of Warwick and was a Jerwood/Arvon Mentee. Her poems have appeared in *Poetry Wales, Poetry Birmingham Literary Journal* and The Emma Press Anthology of Contemporary Gothic Verse. She was shortlisted for the Verve Festival Prize 2020 and commended in the York Poetry Prize 2021. Twitter @ poetryhilary. Hilarywatson.co.uk

9. **Caitlin Kendall** has an MA in Creative Writing from Newcastle University and was shortlisted for the Creative Futures Literary Award, the E.H.P Barnard Spring Poetry Prize 2021, and the Monofiction 'Sanity' competition. She is currently working on her debut novel for Young Adults and a collection of poetry. Her work has appeared at *Fragmented Voices, Alchemy Spoon, Northern Writers Studios, The Black Cat Poetry Press, Bloody Hell Zine, Freeverse Revolution Literature*, and forthcoming at Bent Key Publishing and Writerz N Scribez. She lives in Northumberland with her husband, children, and a menagerie of beasts.

10. **Electra Rhodes** is an archaeologist and award winning writer. Her prose and poetry appears in more than forty anthologies and dozens of journals. Recent work can be found in the Honno Press anthology, 'Cast A

Long Shadow', and in the Parthian Press anthology, 'An Open Door: Travel Writing for a Precarious Century'. She teaches CNF for The Crow Collective, and at various literary and book festivals across the UK. Find her on Twitter @electra_rhodes

11. **Jess Skyleson** (they/them) is a queer, autistic poet and former aerospace engineer who began writing poetry after being diagnosed with stage IV cancer at age 39. They were the winner of the 2022 International Hippocrates Open Poetry and Medicine Prize, received an Honourable Mention in the 2020 Tor House Poetry Prize, and were named a finalist for the 2020 Yemassee Poetry Prize and 2022 Kalanithi Writing Award. Their work has been published in *Oberon Poetry Magazine, Nixes Mate Review,* and *Ponder Review*, among others, and will appear in an upcoming anthology of disabled writers from Stillhouse Press.

12. **Rod Whitworth** was born in Ashton-under-Lyne and now lives in Oldham. He has had poems published in various magazines and anthologies, and has had some success in competitions. He is still tyrannised by commas.

13. **A C Clarke** has published five full collections and six pamphlets, two of the latter, Owersettin and Drochaid, in collaboration with Maggie Rabatski and Sheila Templeton. Her fifth full collection, A Troubling Woman came out in 2017. She was one of four winners in the Cinnamon Press 2017 pamphlet competition with War Baby. She has been working on an extensive series of poems about Paul and Gala Éluard, later Gala Dalí, and the Surrealist circles in which they moved. The first set of these was published as a pamphlet by Tapsalteerie last year (2021).

14. **Sarah O'Connor** lives in London where she works backstage in theatre & opera. Originally from the West of Ireland, she is a graduate of University College Cork. Her work can be found in *Abridged, The Broken Spine, Green Ink Poetry, Re-side,* and *Shooter*. She was shortlisted for the Bangor Poetry Competition 2021.

15. **Claire HM** is a working-class writer from Birmingham, who writes about the possibility of magic in the mundane. Her poetry has appeared in *Tears in the Fence, streetcake, Cape Magazine* and *Coven Poetry*, amongst others, and she was shortlisted for the streetcake experimental writing prize in 2021. Her novella 'How to Bring Him Back' (Fly on the Wall Press) is set in 90s Brum indie subculture, and is a story framed by a spell to let go of the past. It was

also shortlisted in the Saboteur Awards 2022.

16. **Anne Caldwell** is a poet and short fiction writer, based in the United Kingdom. She has worked for the National Association for Writers in Education, and currently works for the Open University. She has recently completed a PhD in prose poetry at The University of Bolton. Her poetry has appeared in a range of publications in the UK and internationally, including *The Rialto, Tract, Poetry Wales, Rabbit* and *Axon*. She has published three collections including Painting the Spiral Staircase (Cinnamon Press, 2016). In 2019, she was the co-editor of The Valley Press Anthology of Prose Poetry, alongside Oz Hardwick. Her fourth collection of prose poetry, Alice and the North, was published by Valley Press in November 2020.

17. **Pratibha Castle**'s award-winning debut pamphlet A Triptych of Birds and A Few Loose Feathers (Hedgehog Poetry Press) was published February 2022. Her work appears in *Agenda, HU, Blue Nib, IS&T, London Grip, OHC, Friday Poem, High Window, Lime Square Poets, Live Encounters Poetry & Writing,* and *Dreich*, amongst others. Highly commended and long-listed in a number of competitions, including The Bridport Prize and Welsh Poetry Competition, Sentinel Literary Journal, Brian Dempsey Memorial Award, Binsted Arts and Storytown. A regular reader for The Poetry Place, West Wilts Radio, she is featured on Home Stage: Meet the Poet.

18. **Dipesh Pandya**, born Dar-es-Salaam, Tanzania, His [im]migrant journey started when aged three, travelling to England, France, America and India. Writing is integral to his practice, exploring critical questions as a Brown artist and activist informed through the constant navigation of intersecting peripheries found within social contact zones. His work merges personal, historical and contemporary material; engaging with processes of [un]learning and sociopolitical discourse in an attempt to find sanctuary from trauma and strength in resistance. Using a range of alter egos he explores chronologies, cosmologies and ghosts embodied in the oral histories of diasporic identity and safeguarding of living archives. Dharti Khoon aur Paani is written by Swan Nemesis, one of the alter egos used by Dipesh. www. handsupifyourebrown.com

19. **Janet H Swinney**: Originally from a mining community in the North East of England, and the first person in her family to go to university, Janet is part of a family that spans the UK, India and the Indian diaspora. As a writer, she operates at the fault lines between classes, cultures and civilisations.Her

stories have appeared in print anthologies and online journals internationally, and have been listed in many competitions, ranging from Fish to Fabula via Ilkley and the Commonwealth Writers' Prize. She was a runner-up in the London Short Story Competition 2014, a semi-finalist in ScreenCraft's Cinematic Short Story competition 2018, and a finalist in the same competition in 2020. Janet's second collection of short fiction, The House with Two Letter-Boxes, was published in 2021 by Fly on the Wall Press. Her first collection The Map of Bihar and Other Stories, was published in 2019 by Circaidy Gregory Press. www.janethswinney.com

20. **Beth Brooke** is a retired teacher. She was born in the Middle East where she spent the important years of her childhood. She now lives in Dorset. Her debut collection, A Landscape With Birds will be published by Hedgehog Press this summer.

21. **Zarah Alam** is an aspiring novelist and poet from Birmingham. She graduated with a first-class in English and Creative Writing from the University of Birmingham and is a HarperCollins Author Academy alumna. Her poetry has featured in *The Stinging Fly, The North, Streetcake Magazine, Ad Alta: the Birmingham Journal of Literature, the Writing West Midlands' Spark Young Writers Magazine,* and *Redbrick* newspaper amongst others. Her debut pamphlet was shortlisted for the Poetry Wales Pamphlet Competition.

22. **Nasrin Parvaz** is a refugee from Iran. Her works explore political journeys based on both her life and collective experiences that she has witnessed and heard about. Her exploration of these subjects started with the realisation that there were no vivid paintings of when she was a political prisoner in Iran. She became a civil rights activist when the Islamic regime took power in 1979. She was arrested in 1982, tortured and spent eight years in prison. Her books are: 'One Woman's Struggle in Iran, A Prison Memoir', and 'The Secret Letters from X to A', were published by Victorina Press in 2018. http://www.nasrinparvaz.org/web/

23. **Kevin Doyle** is a writer and activist from Cork, Ireland. He is the author of two novels – To Keep A Bird Singing and A River Of Bodies – published by Blackstaff Press. A winner of the Michael McLaverty Short Story Award in 2016, his stories have appeared in journals such as *Southword* and *Stinging Fly*, and most recently in the anthology From the Plough to the Stars (Culture Matters). He co-wrote (with Spark Deeley) the illustrated children's book, The Worms That Saved The World. More at www.kevindoyle.ie

24. **Colin Dardis** is a neurodivergent poet, editor and sound artist from Northern Ireland. His work, largely influenced by his experiences with depression and Asperger's, has been published widely throughout Ireland, the UK and USA. His books include All This Light In Which To See The Dead: Pandemic Journals 2020-21 (Rancid Idols Productions, 2022), Endless Flower (Rancid Idols Productions, 2021) and The Dogs of Humanity (Fly on the Wall Press, 2019, shortlisted for Best Poetry Pamphlet, Saboteur Awards 2020). A new collection, Apocrypha: Collected Early Poems, will be published in 2022 by Cyberwit.

25. **Rachel Swabey** is a journalist and mother-of-three from West Sussex whose short stories, flash fiction and poetry have featured on competition shortlists, such as the Steyning Festival Short Story Prize, the Anansi Archive poetry competition and FlashFlood's Best of the Net Award, and in lit mags and anthologies such as Every Day Fiction and Pure Slush. Rachel has just completed the two-year Creative Writing Programme based in Brighton and is working on her first novel. She enjoys quirky, character-driven stories, both realist and speculative, with a particular interest in politics and environment.

26. **Barsa Ray** was shortlisted in The Book Edit Writers' Prize and The Asian Writer First Novel competition. She was longlisted in Mslexia and Fish fiction competitions. She was awarded a mentorship by Peepal Tree Press to work on her novel with Jhalak Award winner Jacob Ross. Her short stories have been published in *Weighted Words* (Peepal Tree Press) and *Present Tense* (Dahlia Press). Her poetry publications include *Magma, Skearzines, Filigree* (Peepal Tree Press), and Beautiful Dragons anthologies (including Saboteur Award winner Bloody Amazing). She has an MA in Creative Writing from the University of Leeds.

27. **Viv Fogel**'s poems have been published in various magazines and anthologies since the mid-70's. She has a collection Without Question 2006 and two pamphlets (Witness 2013 and How it is ... 2018) Her poems and her work are influenced by having been adopted by refugee Holocaust survivors. London based, once an art teacher, involved with community, social housing and education projects, and since the mid-80's has worked as a psychotherapist. Nonna to 3 gorgeous bi-racial grandchildren. www.vivfogel.co.uk

28. **Nigel Kent** is a three times Pushcart Prize nominated poet (2019, 2020 and 2021) who lives in rural Worcestershire. He is the author of two

collections, and three pamphlets: Unmuted, a collection of 32 ekphrastic poems (Hedgehog Press, 2021); Saudade (Hedgehog Press, 2019) his first collection; Psychopathogen, a pamphlet exploring the effects of the pandemic which was nominated for the Michael Marks Award for Poetry Pamphlets and made the Poetry Book Society's Winter List, 2020; and two poetry conversations with Sarah Thomson, Thinking You Home and A Hostile Environment (Hedgehog Press, 2018).

29. **Leslie Tate** is a non-binary author and poet who studied writing with the University of East Anglia and has been shortlisted for the Bridport, Geoff Stevens and Wivenhoe Prizes. Leslie's three published character-driven novels explore contemporary love, changing gender roles, climate/ecological breakdown, and the child within. He/she/Leslie interviews creative and community-active people weekly on radio and online and helps run stages for Extinction Rebellion.

About Fly on the Wall Press

A publisher with a conscience.
Publishing high quality anthologies on pressing issues, novels, short stories and poetry, from exceptional writers around the globe. Founded in 2018 by founding editor, Isabelle Kenyon.

Some other publications:

The Woman With An Owl Tattoo by Anne Walsh Donnelly
The Prettyboys of Gangster Town by Martin Grey
The Sound of the Earth Singing to Herself by Ricky Ray
Inherent by Lucia Orellana Damacela
Medusa Retold by Sarah Wallis
We Are All Somebody
Aftereffects by Jiye Lee
Someone Is Missing Me by Tina Tamsho-Thomas
Odd as F*ck by Anne Walsh Donnelly
Muscle and Mouth by Louise Finnigan
Modern Medicine by Lucy Hurst
These Mothers of Gods by Rachel Bower
Sin Is Due To Open In A Room Above Kitty's by Morag Anderson
Fauna by David Hartley
How To Bring Him Back by Clare HM
Hassan's Zoo and A Village in Winter by Ruth Brandt
No One Has Any Intention of Building A Wall by Ruth Brandt
The House with Two Letter-Boxes by Janet H Swinney
The Guts of a Mackerel by Clare Reddaway
A Dedication To Drwoning by Maeve McKenna
Man at Sea by Liam Bell
Cracked Asphalt by Sree Sen
(un)interrupted tongues by Dal Kular

Social Media:

@fly_press (Twitter) @flyonthewall_poetry (Instagram)
@flyonthewallpress (Facebook)
www.flyonthewallpress.co.uk